Richard Scarry's
Bedtime Stories

A Random House PICTUREBACK®

SERGEANT MURPHY
AND THE BANANA THIEF

Richard Scarry's

MA PIG'S NEW CAR

UNCLE WILLY AND THE PIRATES

THE UNLUCKY DAY

Bedtime Stories

THE THREE FISHERMEN

 Random House New York

989 Pictureback edition. Copyright © 1972, 1978 by Richard Scarry. All rights reserved under International and Pan-erican Copyright Conventions. Published in the United States by Random House, Inc., New York, and simultaneously in nada by Random House of Canada Limited, Toronto. Originally published in different form in *Richard Scarry's Funniest rybook Ever* in 1972 and in *Richard Scarry's Bedtime Stories* in 1978.

rary of Congress Cataloging-in-Publication Data: Scarry, Richard. Richard Scarry's Bedtime stories. (A Random House tureback) SUMMARY: A collection of five stories featuring familiar characters such as Lowly Worm and Uncle Willy. hildren's stories, American. [1. Short stories] I. Title. II. Title: Bedtime stories. PZ7.S327Bam 1986 [E] 86-484 3N: 0-394-88269-5 (trade); 0-394-98269-X (lib. bdg.)

nufactured in the United States of America 30 29 28 27

Uncle Willy
and the Pirates

Not a soul dared to go sailing. Do you know why?

There was a wicked band of pirates about, and they would steal anything they could get their hands on!

But Uncle Willy wasn't afraid. "They won't bother me," he said.

He dropped his anchor near a deserted island. Aunty Pastry had baked him a pie for his lunch.

"I think I will have a little nap before I eat my pie," said Uncle Willy to himself.

Uncle Willy went to sleep. *B-z-z-z-z-z*. What is THAT I see climbing on board? A PIRATE! And another! And another?
PIRATES, UNCLE WILLY!

Uncle Willy couldn't do a thing. There were just too many pirates.

First, they put Uncle Willy on the deserted island. Then they started to eat his pie. "M-m-m! DEE-licious!" they all said.

Uncle Willy was furious. He didn't care so much about the pie. But he needed his boat to get home again. Then he had an idea. He gathered some branches, some sea shells, and some long beach grass. He wove the beach grass into a kind of cloth.

He tied some sea shells
onto the branches and made
a ferocious-looking mouth.

He tied the grass cloth onto the mouth,
then attached some sea-shell eyes.
By the time he tied on a spiky palm leaf,
he had made a ferocious MONSTER!

Uncle Willy got inside.
He was now "Uncle Willy,
THE FEROCIOUS MONSTER."
Look out, you pirates!

The Ferocious Monster swam out to the boat. The pirates were terrified. They all ran into the cabin.

The Ferocious Monster closed the door behind them—and locked it. The Monster had captured the wicked pirates! Then he sailed back home.

Aunty Pastry was on the dock.
"There is a horrible Monster coming!"
she cried. "He is even worse than the pirates!"

Uncle Willy took off his monster suit. Everyone said,
Thank goodness it was only you!"
Sergeant Murphy took the pirates away to be punished.
Well . . . Uncle Willy had made the seas safe to sail on again.
Hurray for Uncle Willy—THE FEROCIOUS MONSTER!!!

How was the pie, Uncle Willy?

You BAD pie rats!!!

Sergeant Murphy
and the Banana Thief

Sergeant Murphy was busy putting parking tickets on cars when, suddenly, who should come running out of the market but Bananas Gorilla. He had stolen a bunch of bananas and was trying to escape.

Murphy! LOOK! He is stealing your motorcycle, too!

B-r-e-e-e-t!

Sergeant Murphy was furious.
Huckle and Lowly Worm had been watching.
Huckle said, "You may borrow my tricycle
to chase after him if you want to."

Away they went . . . chasing after
that naughty thief.

They raced through the crowded streets.
Don't YOU ever ride your tricycle in the street!

They crossed a drawbridge just as it
was opening to let a boat go through.

Bananas stopped suddenly and went into a restaurant.

Murphy said to Louie, the owner, "I am looking for a thief!"
Together, they searched the whole restaurant. But they couldn't
find Bananas anywhere.

Louie then said, "Sit down and relax, Murphy. I will bring
you and your friends something delicious to eat."

Somebody had better pick up those banana peels
before someone slips on one. Don't you think so?

Louie brought them a bowl of banana soup. Lowly said, "I'll bet Bananas Gorilla would like to be here right now."

"Huckle, we mustn't forget to wash our hands before eating," said Sergeant Murphy. So they walked back to the washroom. Lowly went along, too.

When they came back, they discovered that their table had disappeared.

Indeed, it was slowly creeping away . . . when it slipped on a banana peel!
And guess who was hiding underneath.

Sergeant Murphy, we are
very proud of you!
Bananas must be punished.
Someday he has to learn that
it is naughty to steal things.

Ma Pig's New Car

Pa Pig bought a new car for Ma Pig. She will certainly be surprised when she sees her new car, won't she?

On the way home, Pa stopped at a drugstore.

When he came out, he got into a jeep by mistake.
(You should be wearing your glasses, Pa Pig!)
Harry and Sally thought that Pa had swapped cars with a soldier.

Then Pa went to the market. When he came out, he got into a police car.
"You made a good swap, Daddy," said Harry. But Pa wasn't listening . . .
and he didn't seem to be thinking very well either. Don't you agree?

Next Pa drove to a fruit stand to buy some apples. When he left
he took Farmer Fox's tractor. My, but Pa is absent-minded, isn't he?
"Ma will certainly like her new tractor," said Sally to Harry.

They stopped to watch a fire.
When the fire was out they left—
in the fire engine! How can *anyone*
make so many mistakes?

Hey, Joe!
You forgot
to turn on
the motor!

Then they stopped to watch some workers
who were digging a big hole in the ground.
No! Pa did NOT get into that dump truck.
But by mistake, he got into . . .

. . . Roger Rhino's power shovel!
  Ma Pig was certainly surprised to see her new CAR!
But Pa! Do you know how to stop it?

Yes, he did!

Oh, oh! Here comes Roger now.
He has found Ma Pig's new car
and is bringing it to her. It looks
as though he is very angry with that
someone who took his power shovel.

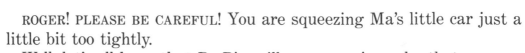

ROGER! PLEASE BE CAREFUL! You are squeezing Ma's little car just a
little bit too tightly.
Well, let's all hope that Pa Pig will never again make *that* many
mistakes in one day!

The Three Fishermen

Lowly, Huckle, and Daddy were going fishing.

Their little motorboat took them
far away from shore.

Daddy said, "Throw out the anchor, Lowly."
Lowly threw the anchor out . . . and himself with it!

Lowly climbed back in and Daddy began to fish.

Daddy caught an old bicycle.
But he didn't want an old bicycle.
He wanted a fish.

Suddenly Huckle fell overboard.
Wouldn't you know that something
like that would happen?

Daddy pulled Huckle out. Why, look there!
Huckle caught a fish in his pants!

Daddy fished some more.
But he couldn't catch anything.
He was disgusted.
   Let's go home," he said.
"There just aren't any fish
down there."

   As Daddy was getting out of the boat,
he slipped . . . and fell!
Oh, boy! Is he ever mad now!

But why is he yelling so loudly?

Aha! I see! A fish was biting his tail. The fish was trying
to catch Daddy. It is good that Daddy has a strong tail.
Now Lowly is the only one who hasn't caught . . .

But look!
Lowly has taken off
his hat. Do you see
what is under it?
A FISH!
Very good, Lowly.

Yes, there you see three
very good fishermen!

The Unlucky Day

Mr. Raccoon opened his eyes. "Wake up, Mamma," he said.
"It looks like a good day."

He turned on the water. The faucet broke off.

"I'd better call Mr. Fixit," he said.

He sat down to breakfast. He burned his toast. Mamma
burned the bacon.

Mamma asked him to bring home food for supper. As he
was leaving, the door fell off its hinges.

Driving down the road, Mr. Raccoon had a flat tire.
While he was fixing it, his pants ripped.

He started again. His car motor exploded and wouldn't go any farther.
He decided to walk. The wind blew his hat away. Bye-bye, hat!

"I must try to be more careful," thought Mr. Raccoon.
"This is turning into a bad day."

His friend Warty Wart Hog came up behind him and patted him on the back. Warty! Don't pat so hard! "Let's go to a restaurant for lunch," said Warty.

Warty ate and ate and ate. Have you ever seen such bad manners? Take off your hat, Warty!

Warty left without paying for his food. Mr. Raccoon had to pay for it. Just look at all the plates that Warty used!

Mr. Raccoon wondered, "What other bad things can happen to me today?"

Well . . . for one thing, the tablecloth could catch on his belt buckle!

"Don't you ever come in here again!" the waiter shouted.

"I think I had better get home as quickly as possible," thought Mr. Raccoon. "I don't want to get into any *more* trouble."

He arrived home just as Mr. Fixit was leaving.
Mr. Fixit had spent the entire day finding new leaks.
"I will come back tomorrow to fix the leaks," said Mr. Fixit.

Mrs. Raccoon asked her husband if he had brought home
the food she had asked for. She wanted to cook something hot
for supper. Of course Mr. Raccoon hadn't, so they had to eat
cold pickles for supper.

After supper they went upstairs to bed.
"There isn't another unlucky thing that
can happen to me today," said Mr. Raccoon
as he got into bed. Oh, dear! His bed broke!

I do hope that Mr. Raccoon will have a
better day tomorrow, don't you?